THE DAY THE TIDE
WENT OUT...
AND OUT...

Story and pictures by
DAVID McKEE

Bedrick/Blackie

New York

Once, the tide went in and out endlessly and the jungle animals played on the beach and made sandcastles.

The beachkeeper kept the beach tidy and flattened the sandcastles. He hated sandcastles.

The animals teased the beachkeeper to make him chase them. While he slept at midday they always built a sandcastle on his back.

But when he awoke, he didn't chase them.

Instead, he walked to the sea and lay down.

When the tide came in, it washed the sand off his back.

And the beachkeeper acted as if nothing had happened.

The animals tired of him washing the sand off.

One night they talked to the sea and the sea chuckled.

The next day the animals were quiet. The beachkeeper
settled down and slept.

When he awoke, the beach was no longer peaceful. The animals were building big sandcastles.

He should flatten them, but first he must get rid of the one on his back.

He went to the sea and waited. The tide went out. He
walked to the edge and lay down. Again the tide went out.

Again he moved. The tide went out and out and out and out, and with it went the beachkeeper.

The animals built higher and higher. They could see the keeper a long way off. They laughed; he could never flatten these huge sandcastles. Now he *must* chase them.

Eventually the sea was so far out that it couldn't be seen even from the top of the sandcastles.

The keeper stopped. He realized that with the sandcastle
on his back the animals couldn't put another there.

The animals saw him returning, the sand still on his back.
At last he would chase them.

But he didn't. He ignored them.

Furious that their efforts had been in vain, the animals rushed back to the jungle and stayed there. The sea, too, stayed where it was.

Nowadays people visit the giant sandcastles. They look at them and wonder how they were built.

The keeper has learned to live with them, like the one on his back. They remind him of the day the tide went out and out and out and out . . .